Coxheath Library
Heath Road
Coxheath
Tel: (Maidstone) 744130

3 0 DEC 2010

2 5 JAN 2013

2 3 JAN

1 7 DEC 2021

Please return on or before the latest date above.
You can renew online at www.kent.gov.uk/libs
or by phone 08458 247 200

CUSTOMER SERVICE EXCELLENCE   Libraries & Archives

C155275292

KENT
LIBRARIES & ARCHIVES

C153971505

STRIPES PUBLISHING
An imprint of Magi Publications
1 The Coda Centre, 189 Munster Road, London SW6 6AW

A paperback original
First published in Great Britain in 2010

Text copyright © Guy Bass, 2010
Illustrations copyright © David Lopez, 2010

ISBN: 978-1-84715-147-6

The right of Guy Bass and David Lopez to be identified as the author
and illustrator of this work respectively has been asserted by them
in accordance with the Copyright, Designs and Patents Act, 1988.

All rights reserved.

A CIP catalogue record for this book is available from the British Library.

This book is sold subject to the condition that it shall not, by way of trade
or otherwise, be lent, resold, hired out, or otherwise circulated without
the publisher's prior consent in any form of binding or cover other than
that in which it is published and without a similar condition, including
this condition, being imposed upon the subsequent purchaser.

Printed and bound in the UK.

1 2 3 4 5 6 7 8 9 10

SECRET SANTA

Agent of X.M.A.S.

Guy Bass

Illustrated by David Lopez

Stripes

Felix Fear loomed over the giant water pipe, a vial of his *Paranoia Potion* in his hands. His ice-white skin glowed in the darkness of the deserted plant.

"HA HA HA! The p-p-perfect end to a p-perfectly p-paranoid p-p-plan," stuttered the permanently panicky villain. "Once I d-d-dump my new super-high-strength f-fearsome f-formula into the water supply T-T-Tokyo will be gripped in t-t-terror! The whole city will b-be as nervous as m-me! Let the m-mayhem begin!"

"Felix Fear – you're on *The Naughty List*," said a voice from the darkness.

"WAAAAAHHH!" screamed Felix Fear. "D-d-don't s-sneak up on m-me like th-that! I'm a v-very nervous p-p-person! Wh-what do y-you m-mean by in-in-interrupting me?"

"Put a stocking in it, Fear. I'm here to bring you in, one way or another," said the voice. Fear saw an enormous figure looming over him in the shadows.

"Y-you! B-b-but that's im-impossible!" stuttered Felix Fear in terror. "I'd heard r-r-rumours, but I d-didn't think – it isn't – it c-c-can't be! You're – you're n-not *real*!"

"Yeah, that's what you're supposed to think, quaky-boots. Now put down the potion, or face the shiny nose of justice," said the figure. He drew a gun from his belt, which immediately began to glow with red energy.

"St-stay back! Or I'll d-d-d-drop this!" said Fear, holding the Paranoia Potion over the water pipe. "Y-you w-w-wouldn't hurt m-me, w-would you? You c-couldn't! You're meant to be g-good! You're meant to be k-kind! You're m-meant to be j-j-j-j-jolly!"

"Rumours of my jolliness have been greatly exaggerated," growled the figure.

Since the Dawn of Naughtiness, the Xtremely Mysterious Agency of Secrets has fought to keep the world safe from harm.

Working out of their top secret headquarters at the North Pole, a team of highly-trained Elf Agents monitors criminal activity all over the world.

The most dastardly and dangerous criminals are put on to The Naughty List – an index of infamy.

Only one man has the skill, strength and big white beard to bring these criminals to justice.

You already know his name.

But if anyone asks, he doesn't exist…

NOT JUST FOR CHRISTMAS

WHO IS SANTA CLAUS?

The North Pole. July 17th,
10:59 XMT (X.M.A.S. Mean Time)

"Umm…" said newly graduated Elf Agent Jingle Bells. He stared at the control panel, shivering in the subzero temperatures of the North Pole. "Wait, don't tell me, I know this one…" Suddenly, he felt a tap on his shoulder.

"Would you hurry up, Jingle? We're freezing back here!" Jingle looked round to see his fellow Elf Agent Candy Cane, and a queue of twelve other elves, shivering behind her in the snow.

"Keep your pointy hat on, Candy – I'm

thinking," replied Jingle, rubbing his chin. "Who is Santa Claus... Who is Santa Claus..."

"The answer is, *'There is no Santa Claus'*," said Candy. "Every elf learns that on their first day of training. Honestly, Jingle, how you ended up on top of the Christmas tree at X.M.A.S.[1] Academy, I'll never know..."

"Yeah, but I did, didn't I? I'm top of the tree, and that's what matters!" said Jingle. He turned back to the control screen and whispered, "Sorry about that. Just clearing something up. The answer, which I totally knew, is, 'There is no Santa Claus'."

VERIFYING IDENTITY...

[1] Xtremely Mysterious Agency of Secrets.

"IDENTITY VERIFIED. WELCOME TO THE GROTTO, AGENT BELLS," said a tinny female voice. Jingle recognized it immediately as *Christmas S.P.I.R.I.T.*[2] – the Grotto's all-knowing supercomputer.

"Thanks, S.P.I.R.I.T.!" said Jingle, as the secret door to X.M.A.S. headquarters opened with a clang and a whirr.

"I HAVE HEARD A LOT ABOUT YOU, AGENT BELLS – CONGRATULATIONS ON COMING TOP OF THE TREE. PLEASE MAKE YOUR WAY TO THE ACCESS LIFT AND WAIT FOR YOUR FELLOW AGENTS," said S.P.I.R.I.T.

"Hey, Candy – did you hear that? Christmas S.P.I.R.I.T. has heard a lot about me!" shouted Jingle, as he strode into the lift.

[2] Secretly Processed Information – Response In Time.

"How *did* Jingle ever make it to the top of the tree?" whispered Elf Agent Mistle Toe into Candy's ear. "He never seemed to be that good at anything when we were at the Academy. I wasn't even sure he'd graduate."

"I know, it's weird," replied Candy with a shrug. "Maybe he just didn't want to show off."

"I don't know if I should tell you this," continued Mistle, "but when we were training, every elf at the Academy thought *you* were going to be top of the tree."

"Yeah … I guess I did too," sighed Candy. "Jingle hardly seemed to know what day it was, half the time."

WELCOME TO THE GROTTO

The Grotto, X.M.A.S. Secret
Headquarters, the North Pole.
July 17th, 11:03 XMT

By the time all fourteen of the elves had made their way through the Grotto's secret entrance to the access lift, Jingle was beside himself with excitement.

"I can't believe we're actually inside the Grotto – this is better than a sack full of presents!" he cried, brushing the last of the snow off his green coat. "No, two sacks!"

"And I can't believe you're not nervous," said Candy, as the last of the elves shuffled into the lift.

"Why would I be?" replied Jingle, a little

defensively. "I was born to be an X.M.A.S. Agent. I love Christmas more than anyone!"

"Jingle, we've been over this. There's more to being an X.M.A.S. Agent than liking Christmas. In fact, X.M.A.S. and Christmas have hardly anything to do with each other…" began a frustrated Candy. "Seriously, how *did* you get to be top of the—"

"Tree!" cried Jingle, staring in awe at a large map of the Grotto on the lift wall. "Hey, Candy, look – the Grotto is shaped like a Christmas tree!"

THE GROTTO

LEVEL 1 - LOBBY, CANTEEN, GIFT SHOP

LEVEL 2 - THE HANGAR

LEVEL 3 - THE FACTORY FLOOR

LEVEL 4 - LIVING QUARTERS AND RECREATION AREA

LEVEL 5 - THE WORKSHOP

LEVEL 6 - THE GIFT BOX DETENTION LEVEL

"NEXT STOP, THE FACTORY FLOOR," said S.P.I.R.I.T., and the lift quickly carried the elves deep underground.

Whatever anyone else might tell you about elves, the truth is they are all between 3'3" and 3'7" tall. They have long, pointed ears, an almost unnatural love of sweets[3], and, without exception, suit pointy hats and the colour green.

[3] Especially chocolate, marshmallows and five-flavour everlasting gobstoppers.

Jingle himself was wide-eyed and rosy-cheeked, with a large clump of bright orange hair on top of his head.

He beamed excitedly as the lift came to a sudden halt and the doors whirred open. The elves stepped out into an enormous circular room, bigger and more impressive than any room Jingle had ever imagined. It was full of banks of futuristic computers and vast 3D monitoring screens.

Everywhere he looked, Jingle could see elves. He'd never seen so many in one place, even at the Academy. Some were seated at computers, which fed them up-to-the-second images and information from all over the globe, while others rushed around like they had something world-savingly important to do. A constant hum of machinery and voices filled the air, and the whole room buzzed with tension and excitement.

"Stuffed stockings! I've been waiting for this moment my entire life!" cried Jingle. "When do you think we'll get to see him?"

"Who?" replied Candy. "Oh … *him*. I don't know, Jingle – I've heard he spends most of his time out there, in the big, wide world – whereas an elf's place is here in the Grotto."

"I bet he's down in his Workshop right now!" continued Jingle obliviously. "I bet he's laughing and making toys and being all, 'Ho ho ho! Look how jolly I am!'"

"Actually, I've heard that he's a bit of a—" began Candy, but she was interrupted by a booming voice.

"Elf Agents, front and centre, on the double!" A chubby elf with an enormous white moustache and a bubble-blowing pipe strode towards the nervous recruits. "My name is Jolly Japes, X.M.A.S. Chief of Operations, but you can call me 'Sir'," said the fat elf, blowing bubbles into the air. "You

elves have been selected to join us at the
Grotto[4] because you are the best of the best
– this year's finest graduates
from the X.M.A.S. Academy.
You have been rewarded
for your hard work with
a heavy burden – to
protect the world from
threats so terrifying that
if anyone knew about them,
they'd probably do a little
wee in their pants ... and
nobody wants that, do they?"

"No, Sir!" came the response from the Elf
Agents.

"But that's not all, by golly!" continued
Jolly Japes. "You have also been charged
with keeping the top-most secret of all the
secrets: Who is Santa Claus?"

[4] 200 Elf Agents staff the Grotto at all times – even
Christmas Day!

SECRET SANTA

"There is no Santa Claus!" cried Jingle very loudly. "I knew that!"

"That's right, by golly – *there is no Santa Claus!* And if anyone asks, that's what you tell 'em," said Jolly Japes. "Now, I know we can't keep Santa's existence from everyone. There's no fooling those kids! But sooner or later, children become grown-ups, and everyone knows grown-ups don't believe in Santa Claus. And that's just the way we like it! The fewer people who believe that Santa Claus is real, the easier it is for him to get the job done. We elves have been keeping his secret and the world safe, for hundreds of years. And we will continue to do so, as long as there are bad people doing things that would make good people do a little wee in their pants."

"Don't worry, Sir, Christmas – I mean, X.M.A.S. – is in safe hands!" said Jingle.

"Glad to hear it – Bells, isn't it? Ah, yes, our top-of-the-tree graduate! Well, Bells,

26

it's just that sort of never-say-die attitude we like here on the Factory Floor," said Jolly Japes, opening his arms wide. "This is where the magic happens. Right here in the nerve centre of the Grotto. From the Factory Floor we can monitor criminal activity and general naughtiness all over the planet, making us the last word in global defence and elfspionage[5]. But more than that, the Grotto is your home. Now then, before I assign you your positions, I'll need to talk you through our Elf and Safety procedures—"

"Elf and Safety? Creased Christmas cards … when do we get to the good stuff?" said an impatient Jingle.

"AGENT BELLS, REPORT IMMEDIATELY TO THE CAROL CHAMBER," said S.P.I.R.I.T.

"That's *Christmas Carol's* office!" whispered Candy. "The big boss – the head of X.M.A.S.!"

---

[5] Like espionage, but with more elves.

"Tangled tinsel! Why would Christmas Carol want to see *me*?" said Jingle, the rosiness suddenly draining from his cheeks.

"There's only one way to find out, Bells," said Jolly Japes, blowing a large bubble and pointing to a thick, steel door at the far end of the Factory Floor. "Well? Don't hang about. You don't want to keep her waiting."

"N-no, Sir," said Jingle, slinking nervously towards the door.

"A meeting with Christmas Carol herself! Jingle's got to be the luckiest elf since Fluky Fourleaf found the very first pot of gold," whispered Mistle Toe to Candy. "What's he got to be nervous about?"

"That's exactly what I was wondering…" replied Candy.

NOT JUST FOR CHRISTMAS

SANTA'S LITTLE HELPER

Jingle stopped outside the thick, steel door, inscribed with the words CAROL CHAMBER.

"GO STRAIGHT IN," said S.P.I.R.I.T. "CHRISTMAS CAROL IS EXPECTING YOU."

Jingle pushed the door open, just a crack, and sidled inside. There, at the far end of the room, was Christmas Carol. She was an old, white-haired non-elf (or "human") lady, with a thick pair of half-moon glasses and a well-pressed white blouse and beige cardigan. She was sitting behind a large desk, looking at a computer screen.

"Ah, Agent Bells. Well, don't just stand there letting the draught in, dear – come in and sit down. How was your trip?"

"Fine, thank you, Sir – I mean, Madam, I mean—" began Jingle, nervously taking a seat.

"Call me Carol," interrupted Christmas Carol. "Now then, I've been looking through your file and I must say, I'm very impressed. Top of the tree at the Academy – straight Xs in every field. In all my years in global defence and elfspionage, I've never seen grades like it," said Christmas Carol, scrolling through Jingle's file.

"What can I say? I guess I'm just ... a natural," said Jingle.

"Well, with these scores you could expect your pick of assignments. You'd excel anywhere in the Grotto."

"Really? Cos I'd *love* to help out in Santa's Workshop! All I've ever wanted is to make toys. A job in the Workshop would be like a hundred Christmases all come at once!" said Jingle.

"Actually, I was rather hoping you'd accept a different kind of challenge," replied Christmas Carol. "Something more suited to your talents. Something ... outside the Grotto."

"Outside? But elves *never* leave the Grotto," said Jingle, suddenly feeling a little nervous. "The only people who leave the Grotto are the Reindeer and ... *him*."

"Not quite," replied Christmas Carol. "Some time ago, we experimented with sending our very best Elf Agents out into the big, wide world. We called it *Operation: Santa's Little Helper*."

"Santa's ... Little ... *Helper*...?" repeated Jingle. "As in, *the* Santa?"

"Well, how many Santas do you know, dear?" Christmas Carol laughed, adjusting her spectacles. "As it happens, the last S.L.H. took early retirement on medical grounds. As did the one before that, and the one before that, come to think of it ... still, let's not dwell on the past. The fact is, we need a new S.L.H., Agent Bells, and you seem to be the only elf who might be up to the job."

"You mean, I'll get to meet – actually

meet – Santa Claus?" squealed Jingle, his pointy ears wiggling with excitement.

"Oh, more than just meet, dear – you and Agent Claus will be working together," replied Christmas Carol.

"Stuffed stockings! This is GREAT! When can I start? I mean, when do I get to meet—" began Jingle, but the booming sound of footsteps distracted him. They quickly grew louder, closer – thunderous, thumping clomps that were so loud Jingle was sure all four of his fillings were going to shake themselves loose.

"What – what *is* that?" he whimpered.

"Speak of the devil, and he shall appear," said Christmas Carol, with a smile.

BA-DOOM!

THE 'J' STANDS FOR JUSTICE

The door to Christmas Carol's office was kicked open. A vast, red-clad giant stood in the doorway. He was *enormous* – a mass of thick muscle (apart from a big, fat belly) and dressed from head to toe in a battered crimson combat suit. His craggy face was covered in a huge white beard and fixed in a permanent grimace. He had a massive sack slung over his shoulder and an impressive-looking gun holstered at his side.

"Santa Claus…" whispered Jingle in awe. He had never even seen a photo of the real

Agent Claus before. From a distance, Santa might have looked like Jingle had imagined, but close up he was almost scary…

"You're late, Agent Claus. We haven't heard from you in three days," said Christmas Carol.

"I had an appointment with Fear – *Felix Fear*," growled Santa, and threw his sack to the ground. It landed with a thud and an "*UMmPH!*" then a long, spindly man with bright white skin rolled out, moaning, groaning, and a little battered.

"Oh, jolly good!" said Christmas Carol, clapping her hands together. "Felix Fear is number four on our Naughty List[6]! You foiled his attempt to poison Tokyo's water supply with his Paranoia Potion, I presume?"

"You m-m-monster! I c-could have s-s-suffocated in there! And I have a f-f-fear of the dark! And c-c-confined spaces! And s-s-s-s-sacks!"

"Put a stocking in it, Fear," growled

[6] A constantly updated database of the world's most dangerous, dastardly and downright disobedient criminals.

Santa. "You'll have plenty of time to get used to confined spaces in your very own cell in the Gift Box. Guards, take him away!"

Despite two Security Elves rushing in to Christmas Carol's office and dragging Felix Fear screaming and stuttering out of the room, Jingle still didn't manage to take his eyes off Santa Claus. Santa was folding his capture-sack back into a pouch in his multi-belt when he noticed the awestruck gaze of the little elf.

"Who's this?" he grunted.

"Agent Claus, meet Elf Agent Jingle Bells," said Christmas Carol. "Your new S.L.H."

"Not this again," sighed Santa. "I already told you, I don't need a—"

"I can't believe it! It's you – it's really you! I've dreamed of this moment my entire life! I'm your biggest fan!" squealed an over-excited Jingle, jumping up. He grabbed Santa's gloved hand and shook it vigorously.

Santa lifted up his arm until Jingle was dangling in the air and peered at him.

"M-my name's Jingle – Jingle Bells," added Jingle, suddenly a little nervous in the face of his surprisingly grim-looking hero.

"Santa J. Claus – the 'J' stands for Justice," growled Santa, and plonked Jingle back on the floor. "As I was saying, Carol, I don't *need* a sidekick."

"And I told you, Agent Claus – you're not getting any younger," replied Christmas Carol.

"Not getting any younger...?" repeated Santa. "I've been fighting injustice since before you were born – by a few *thousand* years. The last Christmas Carol didn't try and foist any sidekicks on me..."

"Now look here, Agent Claus, there may have been Christmas Carols before me, but that doesn't change the fact that I'm your boss. That's the way it's always been," retorted Christmas Carol. "And you may be immortal, but you're certainly not getting any younger. It's not the 1700s any more. You need someone to watch your back, and Agent Bells here may be the one person qualified to keep up with you."

"Fine," grunted Santa. "But don't blame me if he gets ... caught in the crossfire."

"YES!" cried Jingle. "Perfect puddings, this is going to be so much fun – every day will be like Christmas!"

"Don't count on it, elf," snorted Santa, rolling his neck until it cracked. "What's my next mission, Carol?"

"I'm afraid the naughtiness levels have gone off the charts in your absence," said Christmas Carol. "The Reindeer Squadron have been doing their best to fill in, but they don't really have the nose for a mystery, and you know those girls only seem to be happy when they're blowing things up..."

"It's an important part of the job," said Santa, with what might have been a smirk (it was hard to tell with the beard). "So, what have I missed?"

"Well, for starters, there have been some mysterious robberies — it appears that a giant claw has been appearing from the sky and snapping up hi-tech machinery from research labs," said Christmas Carol. She handed Santa a photograph showing a grainy image of a huge, metallic claw. It seemed to be dangling over a building by a thick cable that reached up into the sky.

"Tangled tinsel! That claw could steal every present under the tree! This looks like a job for Jingle and Santa!" cried Jingle, jumping up to try to get a better look at the picture.

"I'm afraid not. Unfortunately, the claw will have to wait for now – we have a more *pressing* concern," said Christmas Carol. "We've been monitoring freak weather patterns all over the world for the past few days." She handed Santa some more photographs. The first showed a town caught in a torrential flood, the next a hurricane over a city, and a third showed a jungle covered in thick fog. "At first we thought they might be a series of odd coincidences," Christmas Carol continued. "Then, two hours ago, *this* happened."

Christmas Carol handed Santa another photograph, this time of a city almost completely engulfed in snow.

"*Snow* … why did it have to be snow?"

whispered Santa to himself.

"That's London, England, at ten o'clock this morning," said Christmas Carol. "Half the city is covered in snow – in the middle of *July*."

"Snow in summer? Ripped wrapping! How is that possible?" said Jingle.

"*Nimbus*," growled Santa.

"Nimbus? What's a Nimbus?" asked Jingle.

"Not a what, dear – a *who*. Doctor Cumulus Nimbus," said Christmas Carol, bringing up a file on her computer. "Nimbus is the world's foremost expert on *weather-warping* – using technology to control the climate. He's quite a clever fellow, as it goes."

X.M.A.S. FILES:
DOCTOR NIMBUS

REAL NAME: Cumulus Cirrus Stratus Nimbus, Jr

OCCUPATION: Scientist; Criminal; Professional loony

STATUS: Missing, presumed somewhere in the upper atmosphere

NAUGHTY LIST POSITION: No longer applicable

HISTORY: After spending the first 12 years of his life in an airtight bubble as a result of an allergy to air (and chocolate), Nimbus became fascinated with that which he could not experience first-hand – weather. After developing a cure for his air allergy at the age of 13, Nimbus dedicated his life to the study – and manipulation – of weather. However, his inability to cure himself of his chocolate allergy drove him insane. He now uses his weather-controlling inventions to hold the world to ransom. And not in a nice way.

X.M.A.S.

"A life without chocolate? That's enough to drive *anyone* insane!" said Jingle.

"It's no excuse for villainy," grunted Santa. "He's just another power-hungry madman. The last time we met I managed to use his own technology against him – and turned him into a cloud."

"Wow! I bet that *clouded* his judgement!" said Jingle. He nudged Santa in the leg, but for some reason, Santa didn't let out his trademark "Ho ho ho!".

"Get it? Clouded?" added Jingle.

44

"If Nimbus has managed to re-form himself, it puts him back on The Naughty List," said Santa, deliberately ignoring Jingle. "And that makes him my problem."

"Quite so," said Christmas Carol. "Agent Claus, your mission is to find whatever contraption the doctor is using to cause calamitous climate change and destroy it. Then I'd rather like Nimbus found – and delivered to the Gift Box before teatime."

"I'm on it. Have the elves refuel the Sleigh – I leave in ten minutes," said Santa, striding towards the door.

"Oh, and don't forget your S.L.H.," said Christmas Carol.

"Yeah! Let's go and make the world safe – *jolly* safe!" joked Jingle. "Get it? Cos you're so jolly…"

Santa let out a deep, frustrated growl.

"You see? I knew you'd get along," added Christmas Carol, with a smirk.

NOT JUST FOR CHRISTMAS

SANTA'S SLEIGH

The Grotto, en route to London,
England. July 17th, 11:38 XMT

Santa strode across the Factory Floor towards the lift, with Jingle scurrying behind him. As he followed Santa inside, Jingle caught sight of Candy Cane at her new desk.

"Hey, Candy, look – I'm Santa's Little Helper! Isn't it great? Merry Christmas to me!" he cried.

"Yeah ... great," said Candy, looking back at her computer screen. On it was the list of this year's graduates from the X.M.A.S. Academy. Candy shook her head, still not able to believe what she was seeing.

CADET FINAL SCORE AWARD

JINGLE BELLS ——► 100% (*TOP OF THE TREE*)
CANDY CANE ————————————————► 97% (DISTINCTION)
MISTLE TOE ————————————► 85% (DISTINCTION)
FUN 'N' GAMES ————————————————► 81% (MERIT)
SNOW BALL ————————————————► 75% (MERIT)
HOLLY IVY ————————————————► 74% (MERIT)

"Bad luck, Candy," said Mistle Toe, peering over her shoulder. "If it wasn't for Jingle, *you* would have been top of the tree. You could have been working with Santa Claus himself, instead of being stuck with monitor duty."

"Well, monitoring is what we're trained for, Mistle – and you can't argue with the scores. I guess Jingle was the best elf for the job…" Candy replied with a sigh.

"So, you're the best elf for the job, eh?" said Santa, as the lift rose to the Hangar level. He strode out into a vast steel-walled space, with Jingle hot on his heels. "Do you think you can keep up?"

47

"I'll do my best! I'm ever so good at wrapping presents, and I know forty-two different Christmas games, and all the names of the— Stuffed stockings! What are *they*?" cried Jingle. Along one side of the Hangar were eight sleek, futuristic-looking fighter planes – each one shaped like a pair of antlers.

"The *Reindeer's Antlers*, of course," replied Santa. "These quantum-jets are the main instrument in the *Rapid Response Reindeer Squadron's* toolbox of justice."

"Reindeer? Wait, you mean the Reindeer are *here*? I've always wanted to meet them! The first thing I did at the Academy was memorize all their names – Dasher, Dancer, Prancer, Vixen, Comet, Cupid, Donner and Blitzen! Is it true they help you deliver presents on Christmas Day? Where are they? I don't see—"

Jingle froze. There, striding across the Hangar towards them, were eight tall, slender women, dressed in fawn-coloured flight suits, with antler symbols embossed on their lapels.

"Is … is that them? Perfect puddings!" squeaked Jingle in awe.

"You can say that again," said Santa, as the squadron strode past, saluting him in unison.

"Morning, Santa!" said Agent Blitzen. "Off to save the world again? The Reindeer Squadron are at your service – especially if you need something blowing up."

"And don't forget you still owe me an eggnog for saving your big red backside in Russia," added Agent Vixen, blowing Santa a kiss.

Santa blushed slightly and cleared his throat. "Keep up the good work, Agent Vixen."

"I think she likes you!" whispered Jingle, with a cheeky nudge.

"I'm old enough to be her great-great-great-great-great-great-great-great-great-great-great-great-great-great-great-grandfather," replied Santa sternly. "Now shut up and get in."

"Get in what?" said Jingle.

"That," said Santa, pointing to the end of the Hangar. Jingle's jaw dropped. There before him was the Sleigh, Santa's state-of-the-art, quantum-powered flying car – four tonnes of raw power, with a bright-red finish and gleaming rims.

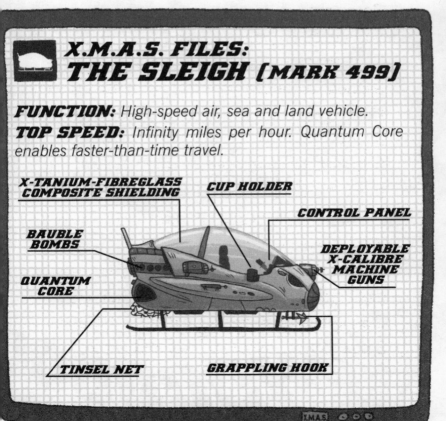

X.M.A.S. FILES:
THE SLEIGH [MARK 499]

FUNCTION: *High-speed air, sea and land vehicle.*
TOP SPEED: *Infinity miles per hour. Quantum Core enables faster-than-time travel.*

X-TANIUM-FIBREGLASS
COMPOSITE SHIELDING

CUP HOLDER

CONTROL PANEL

BAUBLE
BOMBS

DEPLOYABLE
X-CALIBRE
MACHINE
GUNS

QUANTUM
CORE

TINSEL NET

GRAPPLING HOOK

X.M.A.S.

"The Sleigh ... the actual Sleigh!" said Jingle, all but drooling at the sight of it. "Can I drive? Come on, what do you *sleigh*?" asked Jingle. "Get it? Say? Sleigh?"

"Would you just get in?" snapped Santa, leaping into the driver's seat. "And fasten your seatbelt."

"Huh ... there definitely aren't as many 'Ho ho hos' as I expected," muttered Jingle to himself, as he clambered into the Sleigh. In front of them was an endless tunnel, dug out of the ice. Santa grabbed the steering wheel, and hit the accelerator.

"So," began Jingle. "How fast does this thing—"

WHOOOOOO

"WAAAAAA-AAH!" he screamed, as the Sleigh sped through the tunnel. He dug his white-knuckled hands into the dashboard, and felt his cheeks fill like balloons as they burst out into the polar air and zoomed through the sky.

OOOOOOOSH!

"Stuffed stockings! Look at all the shiny buttons!" squealed Jingle, noticing the impressive control panel. He reached out towards an important-looking switch. "What does this one do?"

"Don't touch that," grunted Santa.

"Hey, look! Is that—" began Jingle, his hand hovering over a large red dial.

"Don't touch that either," said Santa.

"And – no way!" said Jingle, reaching for a large, round silver button. "Is that—"

"*That* one you can touch," growled Santa.

"Really? Cool!" said Jingle, reaching for the button. "What is it? The present dispenser?"

"It's your ejector seat," said a stony-faced Santa.

Jingle gulped and jammed his hands into his pockets. He stared out of the cockpit to the icy wasteland below.

"I can't *believe* I'm riding in the Sleigh with the *actual* Santa Claus!" he said, grinning with glee. "Do you know the only thing that would make this moment even better?"

"Yes ... if you stopped talking," replied Santa.

"Nope! It's hearing you do the 'Ho ho ho' laugh! Go on, do it – do the laugh!"

"What's there to laugh about?" replied Santa.

"I don't know – anything! Imagine it's Christmas night. Imagine you've just come down a chimney and found a great big plate of mince pies. 'Ho ho ho! I just love mince pies!' you'd say..." cried Jingle, his eyes glazing over.

"I can't stand mince pies," said Santa.

"What? But everyone knows you *love* mince pies ... don't you?" said Jingle, not quite believing what he was hearing.

"Never have, never will. I don't trust them," said Santa gravely. "They promise mince ... and deliver fruit. They're the liars of the pudding world, and I don't like liars."

"But they're so ... so Christmassy!" said Jingle, scratching his head in confusion. "Don't take this the wrong way, Santa, but you're not quite as jolly as I expected."

"I get that a lot ... but there's nothing jolly about justice," growled Santa. "Now, hold on to your hat – it's *time-riding* time."

"What's time-riding?" asked Jingle, as Santa pulled a lever labelled QUANTUM CORE. Jingle watched in horrified amazement, as the whole world seemed

to pass in front of their eyes in an instant.
He felt his stomach heave, and barely
had time to take off his pointy hat
before he vomited into it.

BLOOORCH!

"Travelling at the
speed of time can be a little rough.
It's not easy on the gut, crossing the world in
the blink of an eye," said Santa, with what
might have been a slight grin. "Good thing it
doesn't last long – we're here."

Santa pushed the lever, and the sky seemed to stretch out like a rubber band as the Sleigh dropped out of the time stream.

"You OK, sidekick?" asked Santa, as Jingle hid his hat under the seat.

"Great … couldn't be better … top of the tree," mumbled Jingle. He looked out of the window to see where they were, but the sky was white with snow.

"Where are we? I can't see a thing," said Jingle.

"According to the GCPS[7], we're in London. It's 19:02 GMT … and I should reconnect with an old acquaintance. Yeah, that sounds about right," said Santa, flicking a switch on the dashboard. "Let's get a better look – activating Sleigh Sonar."

The windscreen shimmered and turned red, and a crystal-clear image of a sprawling

[7] Global-Chronal Positioning System, which tells you where you are, when you are, and gives you your horoscope.

city appeared before them. The Sleigh's sonar scanner was relaying a perfect picture of London. An impossibly thick layer of snow covered the whole city. Cars and buses were already completely buried, and everywhere people struggled to find high ground away from the growing mountains of snow. It was chaos.

"It looks sort of ... Christmassy," said Jingle, peering wistfully down at the screaming hordes of panicked Londoners. "I've always wanted to visit London at Christmas. I bet it looks just like this..."

"So..." said Santa to himself, "if you were a deranged maniac with a weather-warping machine, where would you hide it?"

"Do you think we'll have time to do some sightseeing while we're here?" asked Jingle, obliviously. "There's so much to see – the Tower of London, the Houses of Parliament, Big Ben—"

"This isn't the time to talk tourism, sidekick – we have a job to do," growled Santa.

"It's just, I've always wanted to see Big Ben on Christmas Eve, when the bell strikes midnight. I mean, you can't get more Christmassy than bells—"

"Look, sidekick, if we don't find that machine, hundreds of innocent lives are—

Wait … did you say Big Ben?" asked Santa.

"It's my favourite oversized timepiece, no question," replied Jingle, pointing out the enormous clock tower in the distance. "Did you know it's the biggest clock tower in—"

"Of course – Big Ben!" interrupted Santa, steering the Sleigh towards it. "Sensors are picking up energy readings from inside Big Ben. Looks like a classic Probability Vortex[8] – just Nimbus's style. Brace yourself, sidekick, we're going in."

"Going in? Going in where?" asked Jingle nervously, as the Sleigh headed at full jet-speed towards one of Big Ben's famous clock faces. "W-wait! What are you doing?"

"Parking," said Santa.

KRAA-AASH!

[8] First discovered in 1909 by Professor Dudley Dubious, the Probability Vortex obeys one single rule – it might happen, even if it can't happen.

THE CLIMATIZOR

NOT JUST FOR CHRISTMAS

Inside Big Ben, London, England.
July 17th, 19:04 GMT (Greenwich Mean Time)

"WAAAAAA-AH!" screamed Jingle again, as the Sleigh burst through Big Ben's clock face and crashed into the bell chamber inside! Jingle saw the huge bells suspended above them as the Sleigh spun along the ground, before screeching to a halt. Santa looked across to see Jingle frozen in terror.

"What's the matter, sidekick?" asked Santa, with a beard-disguised smirk. "I thought you *wanted* to see Big Ben."

"Th-this isn't exactly what I had in mind..." whimpered Jingle.

"Well, I think we just found what we're looking for," said Santa. There, in the corner of the room, was a strange, round contraption. It was about as big as a washing machine and made of shiny silver metal. A gleaming blue ball floated a metre above the machine, glowing and spinning with weather-warping power.

"Is that Doctor Nimbus's machine? Candy's going to be *so* jealous – she loves all this secret agent stuff!" said Jingle, adding quickly, "I mean, so do I, obviously…"

"Put a stocking in it, sidekick – we have a job to do!" said Santa, leaping out of the Sleigh. Jingle reached for his seatbelt, but try as he might, he couldn't unfasten it.

"Wait, how does this … I can't make it … why won't it … I'm stuck!" he squeaked, but Santa took no notice. He was already standing over the machine, muttering to himself.

"So … a neutron reactor powering an energized conducto-sphere to create a phase four Probability Vortex. Clever … but not R.U.D.O.L.P.H.-proof," said Santa, drawing his gun from his holster. Jingle watched from the Sleigh, as Santa's pistol unfolded and expanded with a *CLINK-CHANK-VWEER!* to three times its original size.

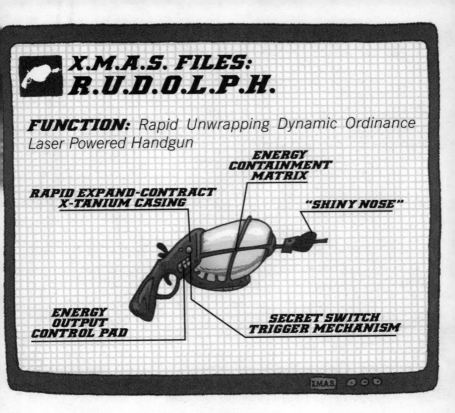

X.M.A.S. FILES:
R.U.D.O.L.P.H.

FUNCTION: *Rapid Unwrapping Dynamic Ordinance Laser Powered Handgun*

RAPID EXPAND-CONTRACT
X-TANIUM CASING

ENERGY
CONTAINMENT
MATRIX

"SHINY NOSE"

ENERGY
OUTPUT
CONTROL PAD

SECRET SWITCH
TRIGGER MECHANISM

I.M.A.S

"Look at that thing! I bet it could cook a Christmas turkey at a hundred paces!" said Jingle, still struggling with his seatbelt as Santa took aim.

"Not so fast, Agent Claus," said a voice, as three enormous figures emerged from the shadows. They were identically dressed in black jumpsuits and masks, and wielding large machine guns.

"Tangled tinsel – it's an ambush!" cried Jingle from the Sleigh.

"Sun, Rain and Fog – Nimbus's *Weathermen*," snarled Santa, as the three giants loomed over him. "I thought I'd seen the back of you half-witted henchmen when I *last* defeated Nimbus. What's he promised you this time?"

"Money!" cried Rain.

"Power!" cried Sun.

"Crisp sandwiches!" boomed Fog.

"The Doctor sends his apologies," continued Rain. "He'd have loved to defeat you in person, but he couldn't make it – bad weather! He figured it wouldn't be long before you tried to dig your 'Claus' into his brand-new invention – *the Climatizor*."

"It creates any weather condition within a two-mile radius – in a matter of minutes!" continued Sun.

"And it's shiny!" cried Fog.

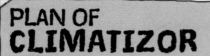

PLAN OF
CLIMATIZOR

©Cumulus Cirrus
Stratus Nimbus, Jr

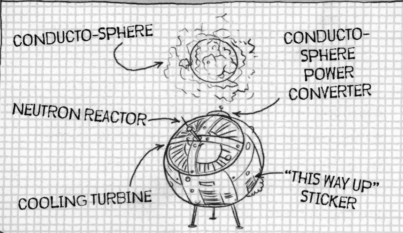

CONDUCTO-SPHERE

CONDUCTO-SPHERE POWER CONVERTER

NEUTRON REACTOR

COOLING TURBINE

"THIS WAY UP" STICKER

"Well, Nimbus picked the wrong weather pattern this time – I hate snow," growled Santa, and set R.U.D.O.L.P.H. to "OUCH" – its least lethal setting[9]. "Now drop your guns, or face the shiny nose of justice."

"I don't think so!" replied Rain. "There's no way you can take us all down, not even with that fancy hand-cannon of yours. You're outnumbered, Claus."

[9] R.U.D.O.L.P.H.'s energy beam settings range from a relatively mild "OUCH" to the blast-an-enormous-hole-in-just-about-anything "KABOOM".

"Broken baubles, they're going to kill Santa!" cried Jingle, struggling to escape. "How did I end up in this mess?" He frantically scanned the control panel for some way to help. "One of these switches or buttons must do something useful. Now, which ones did Santa say I definitely *shouldn't* press…?"

Jingle dithered for a moment longer as the Weathermen closed in on Santa. Finally, he closed his eyes and pressed a button at random. It was large, round and silver. Three words appeared on the windscreen display.

EJECTOR SEAT ACTIVATED

"Uh-oh," muttered Jingle, as his seatbelt unlocked itself.

SPWANG!

BATTLE IN BIG BEN

Jingle's spring-loaded seat launched him, screaming, out of the Sleigh and across the bell chamber.

"*YAAAAAA-AH!*" screeched Jingle, as he soared through the air, before landing with a *KRUMP!* on top of Fog.

"Reinforcements! We've been set up! Blast them!" cried Rain, pointing his gun at Jingle. But as he took aim, Santa fired a single *VOOOM!*-ing shot from R.U.D.O.L.P.H.'s shiny nose, hitting Rain in the chest and sending him crashing to the floor.

70

Sun opened fire as Santa dived for cover. Bullets streaked across the room, blasting walls and bouncing off bells, but after a few seconds, the Weathermen were forced to reload. Santa leaped out and fired, hitting Fog in the arm and sending him spinning into a wall.

"Sidekick! Get to cover!" cried Santa, as a dazed Jingle struggled to his feet. But it was too late – Sun grabbed the elf by his collar and hoisted him into the air.

"All right, Santa, drop your gun, or Pixie-boots here eats a bullet!" cried Sun, pointing his gun in Jingle's face.

"WAA-AH! Don't make me eat a bullet! I'm – I'm not hungry!" pleaded a terrified Jingle.

Santa glanced up at the smaller bells hanging high in the clock tower … and then down at Sun holding a flailing Jingle. They were directly underneath. Santa closed an eye, and took aim.

"The bell of justice tolls for you, Weatherman," he growled.

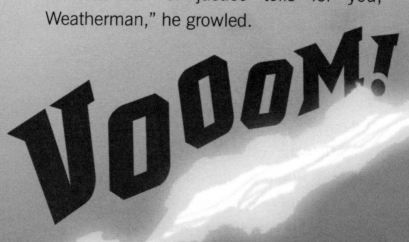

VOOoM!

Santa fired, dislodging one of the bells. Sun barely had time to look up before the bell landed with an almighty BRAAAANG! on top of his head. He dropped Jingle as he fell to the floor, his head ringing.

"Good work, sidekick," grunted Santa. "Your distraction was just what I needed to take down those brawn-over-brain buffoons."

"Distraction? What distraction?" said Jingle, rubbing his head.

"Using the ejector seat to turn yourself into a living missile," replied Santa. "Gutsy move."

"Oh, *that* distraction!" said Jingle. "Yeah, that was – totally deliberate."

"Now stand back," said Santa, turning his attention to the Climatizor and aiming R.U.D.O.L.P.H. "I have to knock out that conducto-sphere to deactivate the machine – *without* detonating the neutron reactor."

"Wait – what happens if you detonate the neutron reactor?" asked Jingle nervously.

"You're about to find out!" came a cry. Santa and Jingle spun round to see Rain, Sun and Fog back on their feet – and donning jet packs! Rain held a small black tube in his hand, with a red button on the end. He grinned and pressed it. Immediately, a panel on the Climatizor slid open to reveal a countdown clock set at:

"You've got exactly sixty seconds before the neutron reactor overloads and *explodes*, taking half of London with it!" Rain laughed, as the Weathermen took to the skies in their jet packs. "I'd say your outlook is gloomy, with a very good chance of certain death!"

00:50

"Cancelled Christmas! Are – are we going to die?" whimpered Jingle, as the Climatizor began to rumble and shudder.

"I've never trusted weather forecasts," replied Santa. He grabbed Jingle by his collar and leaped into the Sleigh. They immediately took to the air and Santa guided his flying car out of the clock tower.

00:30

"I'm really glad we're getting out of here, but what about London?" asked Jingle, as they zoomed away from Big Ben. Santa flicked a switch on the control panel.

GRAPPLING HOOK ACTIVATED

The grappling hook fired out from the back of the Sleigh and into the clock tower, clamping on to the Climatizor. Santa hit the Sleigh's thrusters, dragging the Climatizor out of Big Ben and flying it straight up into the air.

"Wait, now it's right behind us! We'll be blown to smithereens!" cried Jingle.

"Trust me," replied Santa. "I do this sort of thing all the time. Well, more or less..."

"*WAAAAAH!* Drop the Climatizor!" screamed Jingle. "Please, drop it, before—"

"Time's up," interrupted Santa. As they soared above the earth, Santa disconnected the grappling hook and reached for another lever…

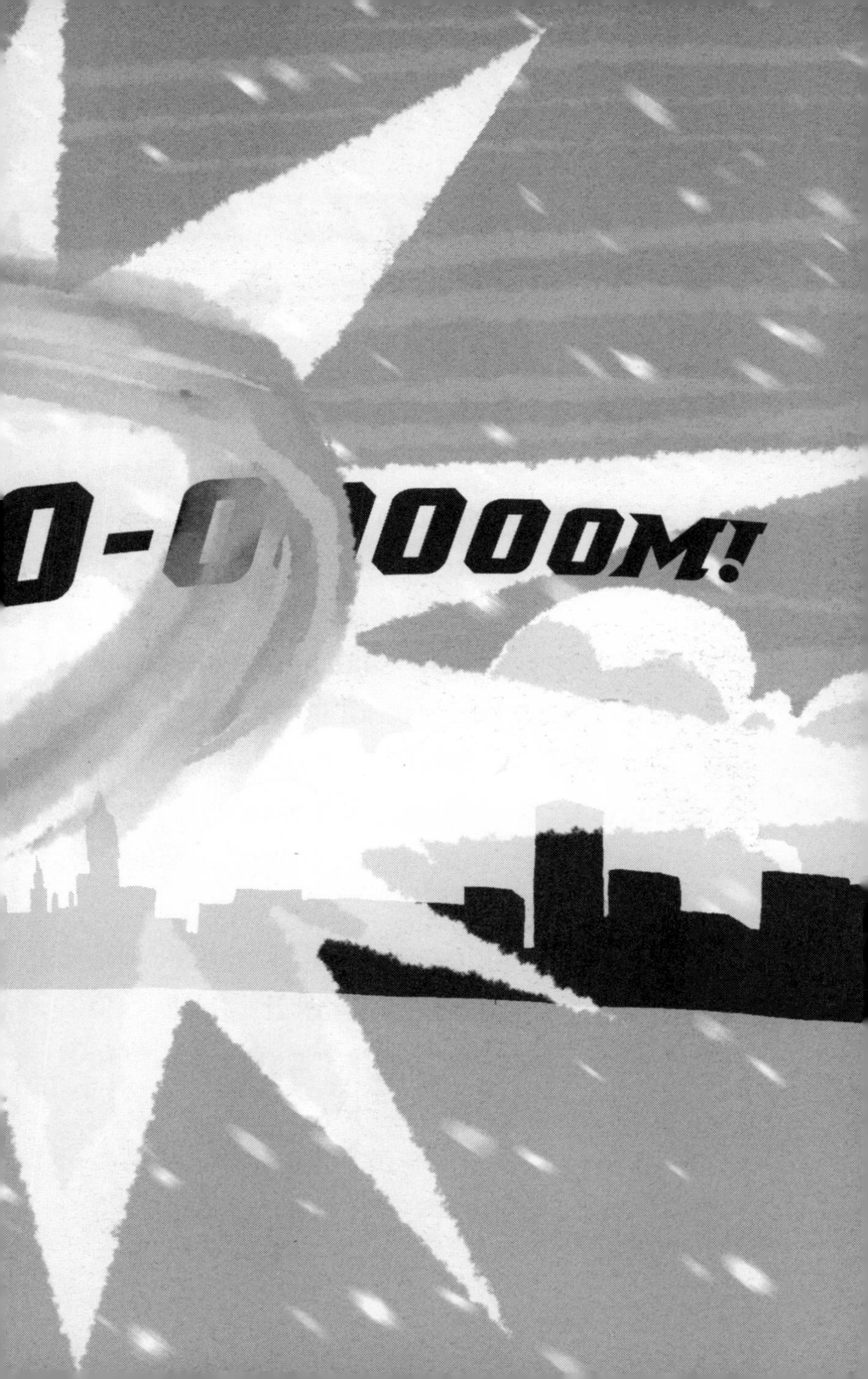
O-O OOOM!

NOT JUST FOR CHRISTMAS

THE LITTLE BIT AFTER THE BIG EXPLOSION

10.2 miles above London, England.
July 17th, 19:16 GMT

"Wh-what happened?" said Jingle, clutching his stomach as he tried not to be sick. In the far distance, he saw the sky light up as the Climatizor exploded high above London. "I thought we were about to go off like a party popper..."

"I told you not to worry – I activated the Quantum Core the second that the Climatizor detonated, time-riding us a safe distance away," said Santa.

"So, we did it... We made it!" said Jingle, more than a little relieved. Then he grabbed his hat and vomited into it again.

"It's not over yet," said Santa grimly. "Nimbus is still out there – and there's got to be more to his pernicious plot than random acts of weather-warping. Why blow up the Climatizor? Unless he's got more than one, or he's planning something else – something *worse*. We need to get back to the Grotto – fast."

"Wait, by fast do you mean—" began Jingle, as Santa pulled the Quantum Core lever.

BLOOORCH!

NOT JUST FOR CHRISTMAS

CLAUS AND CLAWS

The Grotto. July 17th, 12:23 XMT

Seven minutes later, the Sleigh was being refuelled back at the Grotto, and Santa and a queasy-looking Jingle were stepping out on to the Factory Floor.

"Ah, Agent Claus, Agent Bells – nice to see you both in one piece," said Christmas Carol, who was busily popping the bubbles from Jolly Japes's pipe. "How was your first assignment, Agent Bells? Nothing too taxing, I hope?"

"Piece of Christmas cake," replied Jingle, holding his stomach.

82

"We were monitoring you chaps via satellite," said Jolly Japes. "I assume from the explosion that you discovered Nimbus's machine and stopped his wee-in-the-pants-inducing wave of wicked weather?"

"The Climatizor has been destroyed ... but our troubles have just begun. Nimbus is planning something big – I'd bet my beard on it," said Santa. "It's almost as though he *expected* us to find his machine, like he was distracting us."

"Distracting us from what, by golly?" asked Jolly Japes, blowing a stream of bubbles out of his pipe.

"I don't know – yet," replied Santa. "But tracking down that maniacal menace has to be our top priority. I want every elf in the agency working double shifts until we find him!"

"Now, now, Agent Claus – take a deep breath," said Christmas Carol. "I don't want this mission turning into a personal grudge. After all, it's not your fault Doctor Nimbus is up to his old tricks again."

"I had a chance to stop him years ago, and I let him get away," said Santa, clenching his fists.

"You did turn him into a cloud!" Jolly Japes laughed. "There's no way you could have stopped him from floating away."

"Nevertheless, an ill wind is blowing up the skirt of justice – and I'll not stand for it," said Santa grimly.

"Have it your way – I'll set the elves to work on finding Nimbus," said Christmas Carol. "Join me in the Carol Chamber – I want a full report on this so-called 'Climatizor'."

"Sidekick, go and clean yourself up," said Santa, as he made his way to the Carol Chamber. "Then get some food and rest – you're going to need it."

"What? But shouldn't I come along and—"

began Jingle, but Santa, Christmas Carol and Jolly Japes were already halfway across the Factory Floor. "Uh, right! I'll just … co-ordinate the search from here! Yeah, I'll just take a seat here and … co-ordinate…" A wave of exhaustion washed over him, and he slumped into a nearby chair.

"You're in my seat," said a voice. Jingle looked up to see Candy Cane standing over him. She held out a chocolate bar. "Do you want some? You look like you could use a pick-me-up."

"Uh, actually, I'm not hungry – for chocolate or bullets," said Jingle, inspecting his various cuts, bruises and vomit-stains.

"Well, I suppose congratulations are in order, what with you being the new S.L.H.," said Candy through gritted teeth. "How was your first assignment?"

"Huh? Oh, great! Being Santa's Little Helper's the best!" replied Jingle, trying to sound as convincing as possible. "He's so much fun – always cracking jokes and being jolly. Who'd have thought bad guys and big explosions could be so much fun?"

"Sounds *scary*," said Candy.

"Scary? I laugh in the face of scary! Ho ho ho!" said Jingle loudly. "Now if you'll excuse me, I have to go and rinse out my hat..."

"Jingle, wait a minute," said Candy. "I wanted to show you something. I just intercepted another report about hi-tech machinery being stolen – some sort of experimental *super conducto-sphere* was stolen from a research lab in Scotland. Eyewitnesses say a giant dangling *claw* came down from the sky and dragged it away, just like the other thefts."

"So?" said Jingle.

"So, look at the GCPS reading – it happened at exactly the same time as you and Agent Claus were in London."

"Uh ... so?" said Jingle.

"*So*, I already cross-referenced the other robberies with this week's weather-warps. They *all* happened at the same time, Jingle – every time there was a weather-warp, a piece of hi-tech machinery was being stolen. That seems like quite a coincidence, doesn't it? It can only mean—"

"Wait, don't tell me, I know this one..." said Jingle, thinking hard.

"It can only mean there's some sort of

connection between these hi-tech thefts and Doctor Nimbus! Honestly, Jingle, I thought you were supposed to be top of the tree…"

"What do you mean by that? I *am* top of the tree! I got straight Xs in all subjects – you can see for yourself!" screamed Jingle, jumping to his feet.

He bashed at Candy's keyboard and brought his file up on her computer screen. "And in case you hadn't noticed, *I'm* Santa's Little Helper – what do *you* do here? Sit at a computer and stick your pointy hat into stuff, that's what! I probably shouldn't even be talking to you about Doctor Nimbus…"

"Jingle, I'm sorry – I'm just trying to do my job! I thought that—" began Candy.

"Yeah, well *don't* think. Go back to your computer and leave the secret agent stuff to me and Santa!" huffed Jingle. He stormed off, leaving a bewildered Candy Cane standing by her desk.

"What was that all about?" she muttered. She shook her head and sat down at her computer to find Jingle's file still up on her screen. "Speaking of sticking my pointy hat into top secret stuff – let's find out a bit more about Agent Jingle Bells…"

NOT JUST FOR CHRISTMAS

TOP OF THE TREE

A frustrated Jingle hurried through the corridors of Level 4 until he found his new living quarters. He slid his X.M.A.S. card into the slot and the door automatically opened. The room inside was plain but welcoming, with a large bed, table and chair, plus a TV, videophone, computer and brand-new games console.

Merry Christmas to me! My own room at the Grotto… I think I'd put up with anything for this! thought Jingle. *It could definitely do with some tinsel and blinking lights, but still…*

He headed to the bathroom (passing a poster that read "JUSTICE IS FOR LIFE, NOT JUST FOR X.M.A.S.") and gave his pointy hat a good wash. He was just wringing it out when he heard an unfamiliar

DEEP!
DEEP!
DEEP!

"What? Who's there? What's going on?" said Jingle, half expecting it to be another world-saving emergency. After a moment, he realized the sound was coming from the videophone. He rushed over to it and turned it on.

"Santa? Is that you?" he asked frantically.

"Santa? In July? Now that's just wishful thinking!" said a familiar voice. A cheerful-looking, plump-faced lady-elf appeared on the screen.

"Mum!" said Jingle. "How did you know I'd be in my room?"

"I've been calling the Grotto all morning, trying to reach you," replied his mum. "At first they gave me loads of nonsense about classified information, but after thirty or forty more calls they just gave me your direct line. So, how is my little Jingle-Jangle? Are you enjoying your first day? Did you get to make toys like you wanted?"

"Uh, not exactly…" replied Jingle.

"But you were top of the tree! My bright little bauble should be able to choose whatever he wants to do," said Jingle's mum.

"Stop bothering the boy, dear," said a gruff voice, as Jingle's dad shuffled into view. "Just so long as you make sure everyone knows you're the best – that's the important thing. They *do* know that, don't they, son?"

"Yeah, Dad, they know," replied Jingle, blushing. "They've made a bigger deal out of it than I thought they would…"

"So, what *are* you doing?" asked Jingle's mother.

"Actually," replied Jingle, swelling with pride, "I'm Santa's Little Helper."

"Stuffed stockings! Father Christmas himself!" shouted Jingle's dad. "I knew it! A Bells has finally got on in life! What did I always tell you, son? This is what it's all about! Just get to the top of the tree, one way or another!"

"One way or another," echoed Jingle, a little sadly.

"I have to say, considering you're working alongside the world's jolliest man, you don't exactly seem to be your usual joke-cracking self, Jingle," added his mother. "Are you sure everything's all right?"

"I … I—" began Jingle.

"AGENT BELLS, REPORT IMMEDIATELY TO SANTA'S WORKSHOP," announced Christmas S.P.I.R.I.T.

"I have to go! I'll call you later – hopefully," said Jingle. He turned off the videophone and raced out of his quarters.

Wait a minute – Santa's Workshop? Jingle thought, as he sped down the corridor, suddenly getting very excited. *That can only mean one thing – toys!*

SANTA'S WORKSHOP

Jingle took the lift to Level 5. He stepped out into a huge, brightly-coloured room, ten times bigger than the Factory Floor, with walkways, gantries and dozens of conveyor belts snaking from left to right and top to bottom. And, filling every corner, cramming every spare bit of space...

"TOYS!" squealed Jingle in delight. Sure enough, the room was full to bursting with toys of all shapes and sizes. Action figures, space ships, dolls, teddy bears, trains, computer games ... everything Jingle had ever wished for in his Christmas stocking and more.

"I've never seen so many toys in my whole life!" cried Jingle, running into the workshop. He leaped on to a bicycle and started riding it around the room. The other elves ran in panic as he crashed into a giant cuddly snowman, before jumping off the bike and on to a huge trampoline. He immediately spotted a massive box filled with toy cars. He bounced off the trampoline, dug out a handful of cars and sent them zooming across the room, before finding a jigsaw puzzle and completing it in twenty seconds flat. Finally, he grabbed a pogo stick and bounced joyfully around the room until he fell into a pile of whoopee cushions.

PARP! FARP! PARP! POOORP!

Jingle was breathless from giggling when he opened his eyes – and saw the hulking shape of Santa Claus looming over him.

"I see you found the Workshop," said Santa, raising an eyebrow. "I thought an agent of your calibre would be more interested in the tools of a secret agent than the toys we make for the *Christmas Cover*."

"Christmas Cover?" repeated a confused Jingle.

"I'm sure I don't need to tell you how important the Christmas Cover is. Half the elves in the Workshop spend all year making toys so that, one night a year, I can travel the world at the speed of time, delivering presents to every child on the planet. It's such an impossible, impractical, insane idea that no one even thinks it can possibly actually happen. No one thinks it's real, so no one thinks *I'm* real. No one except children, that is … but even they only know half the story. And before long, children become adults, and they forget they ever believed in me in the first place. Even if they meet me, they think

I'm just someone *pretending* to be Santa Claus. It's the perfect cover."

"Wait … are you saying Christmas – the *whole* of Christmas – is just a cover for X.M.A.S.?" said Jingle in dismay.

"Exactly," replied Santa proudly. Jingle stared at Santa in horror and suddenly wished he'd paid more attention at the Academy, and spent less time thinking about Christmas. But it was X.M.A.S.'s fault for making Christmas so brilliant in the first place! As he thought back to how often he'd sat around daydreaming, Santa pressed a button on the wall. Suddenly, the walkway they were standing on began descending to yet another level.

"Broken baubles! *Now* where are we going?" whispered Jingle.

"Welcome to the *real* Workshop, sidekick," said Santa, as they emerged into a smaller, darker room with metallic walls.

It was filled with machinery, weaponry, vehicles and hi-tech gadgets. Jingle was equally impressed, but he couldn't help feeling a looming sense of dread as he spotted a lean, white-haired elf shuffling towards him.

"Agent Claus, how can we be of service today?" said the elf. "Does your beard laser need recalibrating again?"

"You have a *beard* laser?" said Jingle.

"Actually, I'm here for him," replied Santa, pointing at his Little Helper. "Jingle Bells, meet Prickly Pines – out resident tech-elf."

"So, you've got yourself a new S.L.H., have you? Let's hope this one lasts longer than the others…" said Prickly dryly. Jingle gulped nervously.

"According to his file, he's fully combat-trained and up to date on all X.M.A.S. spy gear," said Santa. "I need him suited up for a fight and ready to roll in ten minutes."

Nine minutes and fifty-three seconds later, Jingle Bells was transformed. He was dressed in a smaller, green version of Santa's combat suit, which was so heavy and crammed with gadgets that he could barely move.

Prickly Pines looked at him for a moment and gave a nod.

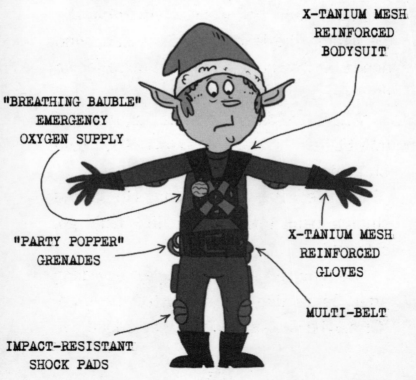

X-TANIUM MESH REINFORCED BODYSUIT

"BREATHING BAUBLE" EMERGENCY OXYGEN SUPPLY

"PARTY POPPER" GRENADES

X-TANIUM MESH REINFORCED GLOVES

MULTI-BELT

IMPACT-RESISTANT SHOCK PADS

"Well, it's not pretty, but it'll have to do," he said. "If you're as good as Santa says you are, this suit will make you a one-elf army. I'm afraid it just slowed all our other S.L.H.s down and made them easy targets."

"*Easy targets?*" whimpered Jingle, trying to lift his arms under the weight of his X-tanium reinforced gloves. "Uh, what say we lighten the load a little? I mean, who needs all this gubbins when you're top of the tree, right?"

"AGENT CLAUS, AGENT BELLS, REPORT IMMEDIATELY TO THE HANGAR," said Christmas S.P.I.R.I.T.

"Justice calls," said Santa. He started striding back towards the lift. "Let's go, sidekick!"

"Coming...!" puffed Jingle, waddling after Santa like an exhausted penguin. "Or maybe I'll catch you up," he added.

JINGLE'S SECRET

Christmas Carol, Jolly Japes and the entire Rapid Response Reindeer Squadron were waiting for Santa when he arrived in the Hangar. Jingle had been so slowed down by his new suit that he'd had to take the next lift.

"Where's your S.L.H., Agent Claus?" asked Christmas Carol. "He surely can't have given up already."

"On his way. What's going on?" said Santa.

"We just received reports of a tornado

heading straight towards Paris, France," said Jolly Japes, refilling his pipe with soap. "Looks like your hunch was right on the button, Claus – Nimbus has got another Climatizor, and by golly, he's already wreaking havoc with it. Why, the people of Paris must be weeing their pants in fear right now!"

"Nimbus strikes again," growled Santa. "But we're still missing something. What's Nimbus trying to achieve with all this? What does he want? There must be a bigger picture…"

"Whatever he's after, you can count on us to help! Our Antlers are fuelled and ready to fly," said Agent Blitzen.

"No, I want the Reindeer on standby here in the Grotto," replied Santa. "We can't focus all our attentions in one place – that's just what Nimbus wants."

Just then, slow-moving Jingle emerged,

huffing and puffing, into the Hangar. By now, he wasn't even sure if he wanted to join Santa on another less than fun-filled adventure. As he waddled over to the Sleigh, he heard a familiar voice call his name. He turned round to see Candy Cane running towards him, carrying a brown envelope.

"Good luck on your mission, Jingle," said Candy, hugging Jingle so tightly he thought he might pop.

"Really? Well, uh, thanks, I guess…" replied a confused Jingle.

"Oh, and I wanted to tell you something. I know what you did," whispered Candy.

"Did? What do you mean, 'did'?"

"I decoded your file, Jingle. I know that you hacked into the X.M.A.S. Academy mainframe … and changed your scores. You *cheated*, Jingle Bells."

"No, I – I mean, I—" blurted Jingle, his cheeks suddenly rosier than ever.

"I should have known when you came top of the tree," said Candy. "You were always so distracted at the Academy – always more interested in Christmas than X.M.A.S. I should have known you could never have got straight Xs…"

"I don't – I don't know what you're talking about," mumbled Jingle, his cheeks so rosy that he thought they might burst into flames.

"And do you know what's even worse?" said Candy. "If you hadn't cheated, *I* would have been top of the tree. I would have been where you are now."

"I – I..." began Jingle, desperately trying to think of a brilliant lie, but all that came out of his mouth was, "PLEASE don't tell! I didn't mean to cheat! I just *really* wanted to be an X.M.A.S. agent – it's all I've ever wanted! But when I found out that I wasn't even going to graduate, I *had* to cheat. But if Christmas Carol or my dad or Santa find out, I'll be thrown out on my pointy ear!"

"That's not my problem. I just want to do my job – and that means getting this to Santa," said Candy, holding up the envelope.

"What's – what's in the envelope?" Jingle asked nervously.

"Proof!" she replied, and started striding towards Santa. "The proof I've been looking for!"

"No, Candy, wait! Come back! Don't do it!" cried Jingle. He knew she could only mean one thing – she was about to reveal his secret! He waddled after her as fast as he could, but his suit was so heavy that he couldn't keep up. By the time he reached the Sleigh, Candy was holding out the envelope to Santa. In a last-ditch attempt to stop her from revealing the truth, he summoned all his strength and leaped on top of her, sending the envelope flying! He watched, terrified, as the envelope spun through the air. Finally, it stopped dead – caught by Santa's huge, gloved hand.

"What are you playing at, sidekick? This isn't the time for tomfoolery," growled Santa, as Jingle and Candy clambered to their feet. "So, what's this?"

"I thought you should see it – after everything that's happened," said Candy grimly. There was nothing Jingle could do – his secret was out. He bowed his head and hoped that the ground would open and swallow him up, as Santa pulled out a piece of paper and stared at it.

"What is it, Agent Claus?" asked Christmas Carol, as Santa's face distorted with rage.

"I knew it ... I knew it!" said Santa. "He tricked us!"

THE MYSTERY UNFOLDS

"Santa, I'm sorry – I didn't mean to trick you – I just…" began Jingle, as an enraged Santa stared at the piece of paper in his hands. He was about to confess everything, when Candy jabbed him sharply in the ribs.

"Ow! What did you do that for?" began Jingle, but Candy jabbed him again.

"Why don't you try *listening* for once, Agent Bells," said Candy pointedly.

"I can't believe I didn't see it earlier," growled Santa. "He tricked us … Nimbus tricked us!"

"Wait … *Nimbus* tricked you? I mean, us?" squeaked Jingle. "But I thought you – I— What's going on?"

"Good work, Agent – Cane, isn't it? This is the piece of the puzzle I've been looking for! Proof that Nimbus's weather-warps were nothing but a distraction in an even bigger plot. Look!" shouted Santa, holding up the piece of paper. It was a grainy photograph, showing what looked like an expanse of sky, and in the middle…

"A balloon?" said Jingle.

"Not just any balloon," said Candy. "You remember the mysterious dangling claw that was stealing hi-tech machinery and dragging it off into the sky? Well, until a few minutes ago, we had no idea what it was dangling *from*. Then, one of our satellites took a picture of this balloon, high above the site of the last robbery. Attached to the balloon is a cable, and – my guess is – the cable is attached to that giant robotic claw. Not only that, but every time the claw was busy stealing something, we were distracted by freak weather patterns, which were happening at *exactly* the same time."

"But what in the name of my stripey underpants has a balloon got to do with Doctor Nimbus?" asked Jolly Japes.

"That's no ordinary balloon … it's a *weather* balloon," growled Santa.

"What's a weather balloon?" asked Jingle.

SECRET SANTA

"They're supposed to be used to measure atmospheric conditions high above the clouds," said Candy.

"Right ... but who do we know that might use a weather balloon in their sinister schemes?" added Santa.

"Wait, don't tell me, I know this one..." began Jingle.

"It's so obvious!" said an exasperated Candy. "Every time Nimbus set off a weather-warp, his balloon-claw was carrying out a robotic robbery somewhere else!"

"Excellent work, Agent Cane. But what does the Doctor want with all this stolen machinery?" asked Christmas Carol.

"Whatever it is, it's bad news," growled Santa. "Christmas S.P.I.R.I.T., run a global scan for any low-flying weather balloons – especially ones hovering over research labs..."

"REQUEST RECEIVED. SCANNING... SCANNING..." said S.P.I.R.I.T. "SIGHTING

CONFIRMED. SUB-ORBITAL WEATHER BALLOON LOCATED IN WASHINGTON D.C., USA, LESS THAN ONE MILE FROM NU-Q NUCLEAR RESEARCH CENTRE."

"Patch the co-ordinates into the Sleigh," growled Santa. "Reindeer Squadron – the tornado in Paris is all yours. Look for the Climatizor in the Eiffel Tower – Nimbus has a thing for famous monuments. And keep a communication channel open at all times. I want you listening in on my every move – just in case."

Santa and the Reindeer adjusted their wrist communicators, and climbed into their vehicles.

"What are you waiting for, sidekick?" said Santa. "We have a balloon to catch..."

Jingle looked back at Candy as he clambered into the Sleigh, and to his surprise, she gave him a thumbs-up. As the Sleigh jetted through the ice tunnel into the sky, Jingle felt as confused as he was relieved – why hadn't Candy revealed his secret? He couldn't decide what was more baffling – Candy's behaviour, or all that balloon business...

"Uh, Santa ... it's not that I don't know what's going on," began Jingle, "but what's going on?"

"Just strap yourself in," said Santa. "It's time-riding time."

"But I just rinsed my hat..." groaned Jingle.

BLOOORCH!

NIMBUS STRIKES AGAIN

NOT JUST FOR CHRISTMAS

Nu-Q Nuclear Research Centre,
Washington D.C., USA. July 17th,
19:05 EST (Eastern Standard Time)

By the time the Sleigh arrived at the Nu-Q Nuclear Research Centre, a queasy Jingle was glad he hadn't eaten anything since breakfast – and that he had brought a spare hat. Santa set the Sleigh down on the roof and leaped out.

"Well, at least my seatbelt worked this time," groaned Jingle, as he struggled out of the Sleigh and toddled after Santa. "So let me get this straight – Nimbus has been making bad weather to distract us from the fact that he's stealing stuff?"

"Exactly," replied Santa. "And I finally think I know what he's using that 'stuff' for."

"Is it something to do with Christmas?" asked Jingle hopefully.

"What? Of course not," said Santa. "Why would it have anything to do with Christmas?"

"I guess I just hoped *something* would be about Christmas…" mumbled Jingle.

"What is it with you and Christmas? Why is it so important to you?" asked Santa.

"Why is it so important to me? *Why is it so important to me?*" repeated Jingle. "The fact that *Father Christmas* is asking me why Christmas is important is just about the worst thing that's happened to me today – and that's saying something! I mean, how would you feel if—"

"LOOK OUT!" cried Santa suddenly, pushing Jingle out of the way as a huge metallic claw fell from the sky and – K-KRAS-SH! – burst through the roof!

Santa immediately leaped to his feet, but Jingle couldn't get up – he flailed around on his back like an upturned tortoise.

"That's the second – no, third – time I've nearly been killed today! I can't take this!" cried Jingle. Then, as Santa lifted him back on to his feet, Jingle caught sight of the giant claw descending through the hole in the roof and into the lab.

"What – what is that?" he whimpered.

"That's our ride," replied Santa, peering into the hole. The claw had already closed around its target. "It's got hold of the neutron reactor – must be piloted by remote control. And I'll bet my beard it'll lead us right to Nimbus!"

With that, Santa leaped into the air, grabbing the airborne claw and swinging himself on to it. He looked down and held out an arm. "Jump on, sidekick – quick!"

"Jump on? Are you crazy? I'm not getting on that! I can't!" cried Jingle, as the claw dragged the giant neutron reactor up out of the hole.

"There's no time to argue – and since you don't know how to pilot the Sleigh, it'll be a long walk back to the North Pole," said Santa. "Now jump!"

"Sweltering snowmen – I just know I'm going to regret this..." said Jingle, and leaped into the air. Santa grabbed his hand and swung him up on to the claw as it floated into the sky.

SWOOSH!

"It's going to be a long ride, sidekick. Use your breathing bauble. Fix it to your nose and breathe normally; the air's going to get pretty thin up here," said Santa. "And try to conserve your energy – we've got a fight ahead of us."

"Merry Christmas to me..." sighed Jingle.

THE HYPER-CLIMATIZOR

Hanging on to a giant claw suspended
by a sub-orbital weather balloon,
somewhere above North America.
July 17th, 22:49 EST

Jingle held on to the giant metal claw for what seemed like for ever, as the weather balloon carried them through the sky to who knows where. They were so high that all he could see below him were clouds. Hours passed, day became night, and Jingle's hands felt as if they'd turned to ice as he tried to adjust the breathing bauble strapped to his nose. Every now and again, he stared up at Santa, whose steely gaze was fixed on the horizon.

"Wh-what do you see?" asked a frozen Jingle, finally.

"An enormous green woman, wearing a crown," replied Santa.

"Oh, that's all right then – wait, WHAT?" cried Jingle. He looked up. Sure enough, he could see the figure of a huge green woman dressed in long robes and wearing a spiked crown.

"That's it! Guns and explosions and puking I can deal with, but no one said *anything* about giant green ladies!" shrieked Jingle.

"That's not just any lady," said Santa. "That's the *Statue of Liberty*. We're in New York City."

"We are?" said Jingle, looking around. In the distance he could see the bright lights of New York City. Below them, on the island beneath the statue, numerous signs reading "CLOSED FOR REPAIRS" and "DO NOT ENTER" littered the ground.

"Typical of Nimbus to choose yet another famous monument," snarled Santa, as the claw floated up over the top of the statue's crowned head. Suddenly, the crown opened and the claw began to descend inside.

"*Please* don't let there be Weathermen down there," whispered Jingle, as the enormous neutron reactor hit the ground with a *CLUNG!* A dozen floodlights exploded into life. They were in a tall, cavernous space, which led from the top of the statue all the way down to its base. Behind them, in the centre of the room, was a tower of interlocking scaffolding. Inside lurked a vast, silver machine, as big as a house, and it looked disturbingly familiar… Jingle gazed down from his perch on top of the claw.

"Tangled tinsel … I knew it!" he groaned, counting *eight* burly Weathermen. Santa drew his gun, which unfolded and expanded into action with a *CLINK-CHANK-VWEER!*

"Nobody move! I'm here for justice!" boomed Santa, leaping off the claw on to the ground in front of the astonished Weathermen. Jingle tried to follow, but his fingers were so frozen from the journey that he could barely move.

"No way! Agent Claus? Is that you?" said a squeaky, high-pitched voice.

Santa spun round and looked up. On the scaffolding surrounding the machine was a large gantry with a control panel fixed to it. Beside it stood a small man dressed in a white scientist's coat. He would have looked completely normal, except for the fact that in the space where his head should have been there was a small, grey cloud.

"Nimbus?" said an unsure Santa.

"Well, well, you are finally finding me!" squeaked the cloud-headed criminal. "That was a clever move, hitching a ride on my giant robotic claw. I suppose I should be congratulating you – you actually worked out the connection between my weather-warps and the thefts. I was not thinking it would be taking you so long! Perhaps in your old age you are getting sloppy, yes?"

"I was busy," grunted Santa. "You weren't the only unhinged maniac trying to destroy the world this week."

"Oh, I cannot be blaming you for forgetting about me. It's taken me a long time to be turning myself back into a human being, but as you can see, I am being my old self again... OK, I'm still having a little trouble re-forming my head, but then my mother always said I had my head in the clouds! HA!"

"That's actually pretty good," sniggered Jingle. Santa shot him a stern glare. "At least *someone* here is trying to be jolly…" Jingle added under his breath.

"But where are my manners," continued Nimbus. "You have been coming all this way to see me and I have not introduced to you my new toy…"

Yet more floodlights lit up the tower of scaffolding. The huge machine was illuminated in all its terrifying glory. It looked exactly like the Climatizor Santa and Jingle had found in Big Ben, but fifty times bigger.

"Cancelled Christmas! That would be hard to gift-wrap," said Jingle, staring up at the massive machine.

"Behold, the *Hyper-Climatizor*!" screeched Nimbus. "My masterpiece, my greatest creation ever – a device of such unmatched power that its power cannot be matched!"

"So *that's* what he was up to!" cried Jingle.

"With you being so distracted by my weather-warps, my robotic claw has been free to 'collect' all the machinery I am needing to complete my device, yes? Once the neutron reactor is in place, the Hyper-Climatizor will be having enough power to devastate entire *continents*! I will hold the world to ransom, and they will be submitting to my demands, or facing destruction!"

"What demands? What do you want, Nimbus?" growled Santa.

"What do I want? WHAT DO I WANT?" screeched Nimbus. "Wait, what *do* I want? Oh yes, I remember! A worldwide ban on all chocolate, of course! My allergy to that unspeakable snack food has been the focus of all my fears! But no longer, yes? If the world does not give in to my demands and agrees to destroy all the chocolate in the world, I will be battering them with cataclysmic climate changes! HA!"

"Not chocolate!" screamed Jingle. "Anything but chocolate!"

"Put a stocking in it, sidekick," growled Santa.

"Sorry! I can't help it, I'm an elf. Sweets are a big deal for me," whispered Jingle.

Santa sighed and turned his attention back to Nimbus. "OK, Nimbus – firstly, that is the stupidest ransom I have ever heard. And secondly, I'm putting an end to your reign before it starts!" He turned to Jingle, still clinging on to the claw above him. "Sidekick, get down from there and cover me!"

"I – I don't want to!" blurted Jingle. "I don't think I can do this!"

"I don't have time to argue, sidekick," said Santa. "Now, get *down* here before –

LOOK OUT!"

Jingle glanced behind him – one of the Weathermen had climbed on top of the giant claw and was right behind him!

"WAAAH! Santa, help!" he cried, but it was too late. The Weatherman grabbed Jingle round the neck, like he was about to snap a twig.

"Got him, boss!" cried the Weatherman.

"Excellent work, Drizzle!" chuckled Nimbus. "So you see, Agent Claus, in no time at all it appears the balance of power is being shifted back in my favour. Now you will be throwing down your gun – or your sidekick *kicks* the bucket! HA!"

Santa snarled with frustration. For a moment he looked as if he was going to attack anyway, but then he saw the fearful look in Jingle's eye and sighed. He flicked a switch and R.U.D.O.L.P.H. shrunk back to its original size. Then he turned and threw the gun far into the shadows. Moments later, Santa and his Little Helper had been tied with thick ropes to the scaffolding surrounding the Hyper-Climatizor.

"I'm sorry, Santa..." muttered Jingle, watching helplessly as the neutron reactor was slotted into place. Nimbus chuckled with glee as the reactor started to hum. Atop the machine, a ten-foot super-conducto-sphere began spinning and glowing with weather-warping energy.

"It's working ... it's working!" cried Nimbus, checking his control panel. "Five minutes to full power! Soon, you and the world shall be witnessing the first demonstration of the Hyper-Climatizor's power – when I lay waste to the United States of America! When the chocolate capital of the world falls, all the other nations will be having no choice but to give in to my demands, yes? HA! But what fate shall I be choosing? Tidal wave? Tornado? Wait, I know – SNOW!"

"Yes, boss?" said one of the Weathermen.

"No, not you, Snow – *actual* snow, fifty feet thick, and covering the entire continent. A new ice age! I'm going to *snow* the world who's boss! HA!"

"Heh…" Jingle giggled, despite himself.

Santa glared at him. "That does it – I've *had it* with the bad jokes. No more Mr Nice Santa!"

NOT JUST FOR CHRISTMAS

SANTA'S SECRET

4 minutes, 11 seconds until Hyper-Climatizor reaches full power.

"OK, sidekick, here's the plan," whispered Santa. "I'll take on the Weathermen, while you stop Nimbus from activating the Hyper-Climatizor."

"Take on Nimbus all by myself? I can't! I'm sorry, Santa, I just can't!" replied a terrified Jingle.

"Yes, you *can*," insisted Santa. "The Hyper-Climatizor is only four minutes away from full power, which means America is four minutes away from being turned into a giant iceberg. Christmas Carol was right,

I need your help," said Santa.

"But I'm not cut out for this!" whimpered Jingle. "I thought I was going to be making toys, not fighting crime! Turns out I'm just a scaredy-elf – I've been *terrified* all day! I'm just not secret agent material ... and I'm not top of the tree. The truth is I – I—"

"You cheated," interrupted Santa. "I know."

"W-what? How did you know?" blurted Jingle. "Candy told you, didn't she?"

"No one told me. I knew from the moment we met that you were lying about being top of the tree," replied Santa. "It's my job to root out naughtiness in all its forms, sidekick. I've been doing it for a long time."

"But why didn't you say anything? Why did you let me come with you and ruin everything?"

"The truth is, I've never met anyone who wanted anything as much as you wanted to be an X.M.A.S. Agent, even if it turned out to be tougher than you expected," replied Santa, with an almost-smirk. "I understand that you're afraid, sidekick. But being afraid is just the start of the journey. Overcoming that fear makes us who we are."

"But I'm not like you! You're not afraid of anything," cried Jingle.

"You're wrong – there's one thing I am afraid of," said Santa. "*Snow*."

"Snow?" repeated Jingle.

"It all happened a long, long time ago," said Santa. "I was just a little boy at the time – two, maybe three, hundred years old. I had a teddy bear called Mr Kringle. I loved that bear; I used to take him everywhere with me. Then, one winter, I took Mr Kringle sledging in the mountains. I knew it was dangerous – the snow was unstable, and my little wooden sledge wasn't much more than a few planks of wood – but I went out anyway. Mr Kringle and I were halfway down the mountain, when I heard a rumbling sound. I looked back to see an avalanche of snow racing towards us! It moved so fast, like it was alive. Just before the snow hit my sledge, I managed to leap up and grab the branch of a tree. But when I looked down … Mr Kringle was gone. Buried for ever in a grave of snow. He was so young, so fluffy, so well stitched. From that day on, I couldn't look at snow without wanting to cry like a baby."

"Huh … I did not see that coming," said Jingle. "But wait! The Grotto … Christmas… You're *surrounded* by snow all the time!"

"Exactly. I made sure that not a day went by when I didn't have to face my fear. That's how I conquered it. You've got to do the same. You're scared you're not good enough to be here," said Santa. "Now it's time to prove that you are."

"You're right – you're right!" said Jingle. "I got myself into this mess – it's time to get the world out of it! But there is just one problem. How are we going to get out of these ropes?"

"Two words," replied Santa. "Beard laser."

NOT JUST FOR CHRISTMAS

SANTA STRIKES BACK

1 minute, 52 seconds until Hyper-Climatizor reaches full power.

A thin laser beam shot out of Santa's beard, slicing through his ropes. Within seconds, he'd freed Jingle and was ready for battle, fists clenched and beard smoking.

"Santa and his little green pet are loose!" cried Nimbus. "Rain! Sun! Fog! Sleet! Snow! Hail! Cloud! Drizzle! Stop him!" The Weathermen raced towards Santa, murderous looks in their eyes...

"This is it, Jingle! I'll hold them off – you get Nimbus! Go! Go!"

"Oooogle!"
FGWOOMPH!
TWiRNG!
WHUMP!
SKYOOF!
"Yerch!"
WHOCK!
GA-DWEENK!
FLOiMP!
"Oowf!"

Santa's fists flew faster than the eye could see. The Weathermen attacked from all angles; Santa ducked and weaved, dodging their blows and crashing his concrete-hard fists into their jaws. But soon, the sheer weight of Weathermen began to overwhelm him. For each henchman he knocked to the floor, two seemed to attack again! In less than a minute, he was buried in a mound of muscle.

"Santa!" cried Jingle, as he struggled to clamber up the scaffolding. He watched as Santa disappeared under the mountain of Weathermen and thought for a moment about climbing back down, but he knew he couldn't. He had to stop Nimbus – the only question was, how? He was halfway up when he came across an answer. There, dangling from a piece of scaffolding, was R.U.D.O.L.P.H.! It was as if Santa had deliberately thrown it there for Jingle to find! Jingle grabbed the gun and scrambled up to the top of the gantry just as the Hyper-Climatizor reached full power.

"You're too late – it has begun!" cried Nimbus. "The world is about to see some *real* climate change. In less than an hour, snow will be covering the entire continent! Welcome to a new Ice Age, America! HA!"

"Your sub-zero scheming leaves me cold, Nimbus! I'm taking you down, *weather* you like it or not!" cried Jingle, wielding Santa's handgun.

"HA! That is actually not bad!" said Nimbus.

"Thanks! At least someone around here appreciates a good pun," said Jingle. "But that's not the point! You're under arrest, Nimbus! Now turn off that machine, or – or else!"

"Are you sure you know how to use that little toy?" smirked Nimbus. "You forget I have encountered your bearded boss and his spectacular firearm before. I know that it isn't activated until you press the secret switch."

"It isn't? Uh, I mean, I knew that! I was just about to ... do that thing you said," muttered Jingle, inspecting the gun. "Actually, I don't suppose *you* know where the secret switch—"

UNGH!

Nimbus leaped at Jingle, knocking R.U.D.O.L.P.H. out of his hand and grabbing him by the throat. Jingle struggled helplessly as Nimbus dragged him to the edge of the gantry and dangled him over the edge. "Stupid sidekick, whatever made you think you could stop me?"

As Jingle felt Nimbus's hands tighten round his neck, he reached desperately into one of his many gadget-filled pouches. He grabbed the first thing he found and shoved it in Nimbus's cloudy face.

"WAAAAA-AAAAAH!" screamed Nimbus, letting go. "Get it away! Anything but that!"

Jingle scrambled to his feet, coughing and spluttering. He looked at his hand. He was holding a chocolate bar.

"How did *that* get there?" mumbled Jingle.

"AHHH! Get it away from me! My allergies! My irrational fears! Get it away!" squeaked Nimbus, stumbling backwards...

"Nimbus! Look out for the—" began Jingle, but it was too late! Nimbus slipped on the edge of the gantry and fell to the floor, landing with a painful-sounding *KWUDDumP!* Jingle rushed to the Hyper-Climatizor control panel.

"How do I turn it off?" he cried. Through the hole in the top of the Statue of Liberty, he could already see snow falling heavily across the sky. He picked up R.U.D.O.L.P.H. from the gantry floor and aimed it up at the conducto-sphere atop the Hyper-Climatizor.

"Come on – fire, you stupid gun! Please, do it for me! Do it for Santa! Tangled tinsel – do it for Christmas!"

Suddenly, Jingle's thumb chanced upon a small button, hidden behind the trigger. He tentatively pressed it … and R.U.D.O.L.P.H. sprang into life with a *CLINK-CHANK-VWEER!*

"Hey, it really *does* have a secret switch!" cried Jingle – and fired!

A bright red laser beam blasted the giant conducto-sphere into a thousand shimmering shards! The Hyper-Climatizor slowly began to grind to a halt.

"Perfect puddings … I did it! Santa, I— Oh no! Santa!" cried Jingle, hurrying to the edge of the gantry. "Hang on, Santa – I'll save you! I'll—"

"Save me from what?" said Santa, throwing the last of the unconscious Weathermen on to a pile.

"What – but – how did you… I thought you were a crushed Christmas cake!" blurted Jingle.

"I was just keeping them distracted so you could do your thing," said Santa, cracking his knuckles. "Eight Weathermen? I don't even break a sweat until double figures. Oh, and good work, sidekick – I knew you could do it."

"You've … done … nothing!" squeaked a newly-conscious Nimbus. He pulled out a small black tube with a red button on the end – just like the detonator the Weathermen had used to blow up the Climatizor in

London. "You may have foiled my plan, but you're still going to die!"

"NO!" cried Jingle, but it was too late – Nimbus pressed the button.

NOT JUST FOR CHRISTMAS

WRAPPING THINGS UP (WITH A BIG EXPLOSION)

"Creased Christmas cards!" cried Jingle, as the Hyper-Climatizor began to rumble and shake. "It's happening again!"

"So it is, you idiotic Agents. I have set the Hyper-Climatizor to overload! In sixty seconds, the neutron reactor will explode, taking us – and the entire east coast of America – with it! And there's nothing you can do to stop it! HA!" guffawed Nimbus.

"Good," said Santa, calmly. "I *like* wrapping things up with a big explosion."

"Didn't you hear what he said?" cried

Jingle, scrambling down the scaffolding as fast as he could. "That thing's going to blow us into a million pieces! Even if we had the Sleigh, there's no way we could lift it!"

"Have a little faith, sidekick," said Santa, pressing a button on his wrist communicator. "Claus to Reindeer Squadron: I trust you've been listening in. Where are you? The turkey is ready to be taken out of the oven."

"Blitzen to Santa – sorry about the delay, it took us a little longer than we thought dealing with that pesky tornado. Still, better twelve seconds late than never – look up."

Santa, Jingle and Nimbus all peered out of the open top of the statue to see eight sleek, Antler-shaped fighter jets appear in the sky above them.

"The Reindeer!" cried Jingle. "They're here!"

X.M.A.S. FILES:
THE REINDEERS' ANTLERS

FUNCTION: *Quantum-powered Jet Fighters, piloted by the all-female RAPID RESPONSE REINDEER SQUADRON – Agents DASHER, DANCER, PRANCER, VIXEN, COMET, CUPID, DONNER and BLITZEN*

TOP SPEED: *Infinity miles per hour. Quantum Core enables faster-than-time travel.*

FRICTIONLESS X-TANIUM COMPOSITE HULL

PINE-SCENTED AIR FRESHENER

PILOT SEAT

FRONT MOUNTED X-CALIBRE MACHINE

GRAPPLING HOOK

REAR MOUNTED X-CALIBRE MACHINE

QUANTUM CORE

NAUGHTINESS-SEEKING MISSILES

X.M.A.S.

"I'd say your timing is perfect, Agent Blitzen," said Santa. "Now fix your grappling hooks to this thing and haul away. You've got exactly 30 seconds before you need to de-clamp and time-ride out of there."

155

"Message received and understood," replied Blitzen. "Now if you wouldn't mind clearing the area…"

"Roger that," replied Santa, grabbing hold of Nimbus. "Sidekick, since you're such a good shot with R.U.D.O.L.P.H., would you do the honours and make us an exit?" asked Santa.

"Don't mind if I do!" said Jingle, aiming R.U.D.O.L.P.H.'s shiny nose at a nearby wall.

He changed the setting to

"KABOOM"

and…

The laser blasted a giant hole in the wall! Santa hurled the unconscious Weathermen through the hole one by one, while Jingle prodded Nimbus with his chocolate bar until they were both outside and clear of the statue. As the Reindeer Squadron began to haul the Hyper-Climatizor out of the statue,

SECRET SANTA

Santa leaped through the gap, a split second before the scaffolding crashed to the ground. The eight Antlers soared into the sky, carrying the Hyper-Climatizor with them. After only a few moments, it disappeared into the darkness. Then, five short seconds later…

The sky lit up as the Hyper-Climatizor exploded into a billion-and-two pieces!

"Nooooooo!" screamed Nimbus. "My machine! My precious, calamity-causing machine!"

"Oh, put a stocking in it, Nimbus – unless you want another dose of chocolate," said Jingle. Nimbus shrank with terror. "Do you think they made it?" added Jingle, turning to Santa. Santa upped the volume on his communicator.

"Tell your S.L.H. not to worry, Santa – all Reindeer are present and accounted for," said Agent Blitzen.

"Good work, Agents. I knew you'd *weather* the storm..." replied Santa.

"Hey, you made a *joke*," said Jingle. "That was almost ... jolly!"

NOT A BAD
DAY'S WORK

One short trip later (which included a stop-off to collect the Sleigh, a trip to the local police department to drop off Nimbus's Weathermen and two-and-a-half not-quite vomits on Jingle's part), the Reindeer Squadron, Jingle and Santa (with Nimbus slung over his shoulder in a capture-sack) made their way to the Factory Floor. Christmas Carol, Jolly Japes and the elves were all waiting for them. A cheer went up as they stepped out of the lift.

"You hear that, Nimbus? That's what

justice sounds like," said Santa, handing the sack to two Security Elves. "I'm sure it'll ring in your ears when you're languishing in your Gift Box cell."

"You haven't seen the last of me, Santa Claus!" cried Nimbus from inside the sack, as he was carried away.

You'll see! I will be having my revenge! I will be having my reveeeeeeenge!

"Well done, Agents!" said a delighted Christmas Carol. "The world is saved and another villain is ticked off The Naughty List. I'd say that's not a bad day's work."

As everyone congratulated each other on a job well done, Jingle felt a tap on his shoulder. He turned to see Candy Cane.

"So, did you get my little present? I dropped it into one of your belt pouches when I gave you a hug," said Candy. "I had a feeling you might come up against Nimbus, so I thought a chocolate bar might come in handy..."

"That was you? I just assumed chocolate was a standard-issue snack!" gasped Jingle. "Thanks, Candy – you saved my life! But why, after you found out I cheated?"

"Yeah, I *was* pretty angry with you about that," admitted Candy, adjusting her pointy hat. "Especially after I found out *I* was supposed to be top of the tree. But when

I saw how you were after your assignment, do you know what I realized? I don't *want* to be Santa's Little Helper – it's too much for any elf! I just want to do my job, here at the Grotto. So don't worry, your secret is safe with me."

"Oh, my secret's well and truly out – Santa knows I cheated," sighed Jingle. "Anyway, it's time I faced up to the fact I'm just not cut out for life in X.M.A.S. Time to head home to Greendale Wood…"

"Actually, I think you more than earned a place in the Agency," said a voice. Jingle turned to see Santa standing over him. "I was thinking of offering you a place in my Workshop, since I know that's what you really want."

"The Workshop? Making toys? Really? But that would be great! That would be perfect! That would be … better than Christmas!" cried Jingle.

"Excellent – then all's well that ends well," said Christmas Carol. "And I think you all deserve to put your feet up for a while."

"Justice never rests," said Santa grimly, then he stroked his beard thoughtfully. "But OK, maybe just for ten minutes."

"INCOMING TRANSMISSION ON FREQUENCY X!" said Christmas S.P.I.R.I.T. loudly. "STANDBY TO RECEIVE..."

"Frequency X? That's our top-secret frequency! No one knows about that outside the Agency!" cried Jolly Japes.

Every computer screen and monitor on the Factory Floor flickered and went black. A moment later, they were filled with the same image – a pumpkin-headed man, with a hideous, evil-looking face, illuminated from inside.

"Attention, world!" said the pumpkin man. "I am Lantern Jack, and I interrupt your regular programming to bring you this message. For centuries, the forces of order and justice have kept my kind at bay. But no longer! Now begins the age of H.A.L.L.O.W.E.E.N. – the *Hateful Agents of Larceny, Loathing, Odiousness, Wickedness, Evil and Even Nonsense*! The age of chaos, fear and madness is about to begin! You have two choices – trick or treat! Pay us ten billion dollars, or we will play a trick on the world – the sort of trick that will make even the bravest among you do a little wee in your pants!"

"The fiends!" cried Jolly Japes.

"You have one hour. So, what's it to be – trick or treat?" hissed Lantern Jack. His image faded from the screens and power returned to the Factory Floor. Jingle shuddered with fear. At least if the world fell into chaos, he'd be in the safest place, locked away in the Workshop making toys. But suddenly, for some strange reason, that didn't seem like enough...

"Ready the Sleigh – Lantern Jack just made it to the top of The Naughty List," said Santa.

"But how will you find him, by golly?" asked Jolly Japes.

"I'll follow my nose," growled Santa, striding towards the lift. "Justice will lead the way!"

"Santa, wait!" cried Jingle, racing after him.

"What is it, Jingle?" asked Santa, holding

the lift doors. "I can't keep justice waiting."

"Actually – and I can't believe I'm saying this – I was wondering if the position of Santa's Little Helper was still available. That is, if you think I'm up to it…"

"Do *you* think you're up to it?" asked Santa, putting his hand on Jingle's shoulder.

"I don't know – but I'll try to be," replied Jingle. Santa paused for a moment, and let out a little grunt.

"Then let's go – sidekick."

"Plus, let's face it anyway, you need me," said Jingle, rushing into the lift. "I mean, someone's got to try and get a laugh out of you! After all, it's all in a good *Claus*! Get it? Cause? Claus?"

"Ho ho ho," said Santa, with an almost definite smile!

X.M.

CHAIN OF COMMAND

DIRECTOR GENERAL:

Christmas Carol

CHIEF OF OPERATIONS:

Jolly Japes

WORKSHOP CO-ORDINATOR:

Prickly Pines

A.S.

RAPID RESPONSE REINDEER SQUADRON:

Dasher, Dancer, Prancer, Vixen, Comet, Cupid, Donner and Blitzen

ELF AGENTS:

(200 active in the Grotto at all times)

THERE IS NO SANTA CLAUS

THE NAUGHTY LIST

TOP 10

1] DOCTOR CUMULUS NIMBUS
   (RE-ENTRY)

2] ANNA NIMITY

3] THE TOOTH FAIRY

4] FELIX FEAR

5] THE TEMPUS FUGITIVES

6] IAN VIDIOUS

7] GNAWS

8] COLDFINGER

9] DR DINOSAUR

10] THE EASTER BUNNY